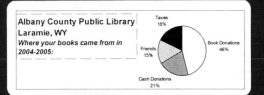

for Kees Heij and Henk de Jong: sources of inspiration

Copyright © 2005 by Lemniscaat b.v. Rotterdam
Originally published in the Netherlands
by Lemniscaat b.v. Rotterdam under the title *Kriebelpoten*
All rights reserverd
Printed in Belgium
CIP data available
First U.S. edition

*The English edition of this book has been made possible with
financial support from the Foundation for the Production
and Translation of Dutch Literature.*

Creepy Crawlies

Hans Post & Irene Goede

translated by Nancy Forest-Flier

Front Street ❧ Lemniscaat

Everyone in the big house is still asleep.
You can hear the sounds of snoring from
the big bedroom.
In the little girl's room a clock is ticking.
Otherwise the house is quiet. Very quiet.
In the living room there's an armchair,
and sitting there is a young cat.
Her name is Lika. A fly is zooming
around her head...

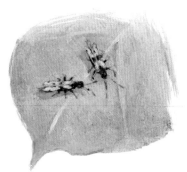

the housefly with maggots and a pupa

The **housefly** lays its eggs in manure and kitchen scraps. When each egg hatches, a maggot comes out. After eating its fill the maggot makes a hard covering around its body. Inside the covering it turns into a fly. A housefly likes to eat bread and jam, but it also likes to sit on poop. That's why it's a good idea to keep the flies off your sandwich. There are different kinds of flies living in the house. The small housefly is the kind that keeps flying around lamps. The fly with the green body is a green blowfly. The blue blowfly is also called a bluebottle fly.

In the summer you sometimes see little black-and-white-striped insects flying around. These are **thrips**, and if you see one there are sure to be many more. Some come in the house and drink the sap from the plants. Sometimes thrips bite people, too. Their bites can be itchy. Thrips don't live very long in the house. It's usually not damp enough, so they dry out and die. Thrips can jump, just like fleas.

Crane flies are very large mosquitoes with long legs. At night they fly into the bedroom or bathroom if the light is on and the window is open. You don't have to be afraid of them, because they don't sting. The larva of the crane fly loves to eat plants. It's hard to imagine such a fat, stuffed larva turning into a skinny mosquito!

Cats and dogs are sometimes infested with **fleas**. When that happens they scratch all the time, because fleas itch. It's the flea bite that itches so much. The saliva from the flea gets under the animal's skin, and that's what gives the dog or cat such an itchy feeling. Some fleas can jump almost twelve inches – two hundred times their body length. If you were to jump that far, it would be a 115-foot jump! Human fleas exist, too, but they're rare. Our houses are far too dry and too clean for those little jumpers.

If you shake out a rug or vacuum the carpet, you may suddenly loosen up all sorts of things. Maybe there are **carpet beetles** in your living room. They love a tasty bit of carpet, and they don't leave many leftovers. The larvae of the beetles are the culprits. They'll eat anything. Are there any stuffed animals in your house? It's one of their favorite foods! A fur coat? There won't be anything left but bare skin. The fur beetle can do quite a bit of damage, too. You can tell a **fur beetle** by the white spots on its carapace.

Wherever people are living you'll find the **house mouse**. It's very adaptable and lives in warm and cold climates, in sheds and in apartments, in boats and on farms. In the summer the house mouse lives outside, too, but when fall comes it prefers a roof over its head.

A house mouse needs only two things: food and a dry place to build a nest. It eats almost everything and has a good sense of smell. It builds its nest with whatever it can find: plastic, clothes, old newspapers or bits of yarn. A house mouse can bear young five to ten times a year.

If there's enough food nearby, hundreds of house mice can be born in one year's time.

Daddy longlegs look like spiders, but they're not. They have only two eyes, and spiders have six or eight. Daddy longlegs walk around the house at night searching for food. They don't spin webs; they use their sense of touch to hunt for food. If they run into something edible, they grab it with their legs. Then they bite the prey into pieces and chew it up. They suck out the juice and spit out the skin. The legs of the daddy longlegs easily become detached if it is attacked. A detached leg keeps on moving to attract attention. That way the daddy longlegs can quickly escape – minus one leg...

Fruit flies are very tiny and have little red eyes. You often see them on ripe fruit. Set out a bowl of fruit for two weeks and the fruit flies are sure to find it. They drink the fruit sap and lay their eggs inside. If you pick up a rotting apple or an overripe banana from the bowl, a cloud of fruit flies will fly up.

Cockroaches live in houses that aren't very clean. They hide during the day and come out at night to search for food. You can take cockroaches home with you without even knowing it. If you step on an egg case, it'll stick to your shoe. When you get home the egg case will loosen and the eggs will come out. If there's enough food, the cockroaches will make themselves at home in your house. After six months they'll be full grown, and before you know it you'll have a plague of cockroaches.

Dark-colored beetles fly around at night in search of food. They fly inside through open windows. These darkling beetles are searching for open sacks of grain or bags of flour. You won't find them in the kitchen because the house isn't damp enough for them. Darkling beetles used to live in bakeries and places where grain was stored. The **mealworm** is more common than the darkling beetle. Actually it's not a worm at all; it's the larva of the darkling beetle. Mealworms are bred as food for caged birds and reptiles.

a mealworm is the larva of a darkling beetle

The fly is in the kitchen. Lika runs after it.
She jumps up to catch the fly, but it escapes
through the open window. Lika lands on
the garbage can. Oops...the garbage can
falls over. Big brown beetles run every
which way. Cockroaches!

The bedroom door is open and Lika slips inside. She crawls under the bed, pricks up her ears and listens. Smack! The little girl slaps her cheek and snuggles down quickly under the covers. A mosquito is trying to bite her. Lika jumps up and runs back downstairs in a flash.

Female **mosquitoes** lay their eggs in water. But before they do, they bite a person or an animal and fill their bellies with blood. The blood makes the eggs grow. The eggs in the water produce larvae, and later the larvae become mosquitoes. The males don't bite. In the fall you sometimes see larger mosquitoes in the house. This isn't the same kind that bites you in the summer. Usually you don't see any mosquitoes in the winter. They're there, but they're hibernating. If they wake up, they can bite you in the winter, too.

Clothes moths are small butterflies. There are many different kinds of clothes moths, and they all look alike. A box with old clothes or a rolled-up carpet is all these moths need. They lay their eggs there, and the larvae eat the wool. The larvae spin cocoons around themselves so they won't dry out. They make the cocoons from the wool that they chew from the carpet or from an old sweater. Sometimes they even use their own excrement. It has to be damp enough in a house or the larvae will die.

If you see a **silverfish** it's usually just for a second. You might turn on the bathroom light and see something shoot away in a flash. It could be a silverfish, surprised by the light and trying to find a safe place. Silverfish can live only in damp places, like the bathroom. They can live a long time – sometimes five years. Silverfish have existed on earth for ages. They were here before the dinosaurs. They don't lay many eggs – no more than twenty in their whole lifetime.

You don't see **mites** very often. That's because they're so small; most mites are no bigger than a pinhead. Adult mites have eight legs, just like spiders. They have no wings. Some are a dull shade of gray, but there are others with brilliant colors. The **dust mite** can be found in many houses. It thrives in dampness and warmth and eats the flakes of skin that fall off our bodies. Don't be shocked, but this mite usually lives in beds...

The **bedbug** hides in beds, too. As soon as it's dark and there's someone lying in the bed, the bedbug gets started. It searches for the warm body and jabs it with its proboscis. An adult bedbug can drink five times its body weight in blood. Fortunately the bedbug is very small and only drinks a few drops... Bedbugs live only in houses where it's really very dirty.

Lika is walking on the terrace. There are plenty of insects outside, even though it's still early. Butterflies flutter among the flowers, bees search for nectar and pollen. Little insects scamper across the paving stones: ants...

*cabbage butterfly and
cabbage butterfly caterpillar*

Cabbage butterflies can be found everywhere. The caterpillars live on different kinds of cabbage, which is how the butterfly gets its name. Cabbage butterflies can be seen in the garden early in the year. They hibernate as chrysalises. These lay eggs, and when the eggs hatch, new cabbage butterflies come out that can be seen later in the year. You might see cabbage butterflies flying around in the late fall. There are two kinds: small and large.

Honeybees can be found in almost every garden. They come there in search of nectar and pollen. Nectar is found in flowers. The bees suck out the sticky substance with their proboscis. They sweep up the pollen from the stamens with their back legs and form it into little yellow balls. Then they take the food to the hive, where they pass it on to other bees. These bees take the food to the larvae in the hive. Honeybees tell each other where the food can be found. If a bee has discovered a good food source, it dances for the other bees by shaking the back of its body and walking around in figure eights. In this way it lets the others know where to fly.

Sometimes you come across **wood lice** in damp places in the garden, and sometimes in the house, too. Wood lice quickly go into hiding when they're disturbed. You find them in many different colors. A wood louse is not an insect. It comes from the same family as the crab and the lobster. The females carry their eggs in an egg pouch under their body. They breathe by means of gills, which are located on the hind feet and on the head. If a wood louse strays into the living room it's in big trouble. It will dry out within just a few hours. Wood lice eat plants, but they also gnaw on dead animals.

Carpenter ants are never alone. They live with thousands of other ants in big colonies in the ground or under paving stones. In each colony you'll find workers, males, and one or more queens. The workers search for food. They eat other insects, but they also eat anything sweet. If they come across something tasty they tell each other where to find it. It won't be long before a whole row of ants shows up to eat. The queens and males are born in the summer. They all have wings. They crawl outside and mate in the air. When they're back on the ground the wings fall off and the young queens crawl underground. There they start a new colony. The males quickly die off.

You can tell **wasps** by their yellow and black stripes. In April the queen wakes up. She's been sleeping all winter long. First she gets something to eat, and then she searches for a place to build her nest. She builds it from finely chewed wood chips and lays about ten eggs inside. Each egg gets a room of its own. The young that hatch help her finish building the nest. They also catch flies and butterflies, which they chew up fine and feed to the larvae. At the end of the year all the wasps die, except for the queen. She looks for a quiet place to hibernate.

Long blades of grass tickle Lika's belly.
Boing! Up jumps a grasshopper right before
her eyes. Lika sneaks closer, but the grasshopper shoots off and lands near the pond.
The ground near the pond is soft, and Lika's
legs sink in. Yuck! She doesn't like having
dirty feet. But that's not the worst of it: Lika
loses her footing and falls in the pond.

Urban pigeons are tame pigeons. They live on garbage and sometimes people feed them. Urban pigeons live in large groups. Before they brood they form pairs. The male puts on quite a show for the females. He puffs himself up and distends his throat. Most urban pigeons brood on balconies in very simple nests. They make a huge mess there and coo for hours on end. Not so nice if it's your balcony.

A **tick** has tons of patience. It waits for days until an animal walks beneath it; then it drops down and holds on tight. The tick crawls to the animal's skin along the shafts of hair. Then it sticks its proboscis in. It sucks out blood and grows to ten times its original size. When it's had enough to drink, it drops onto the grass.

You see **starlings** in the garden all year round, yet they're not always the same starlings. In the winter lots of other starlings fly in from far away. They spend the winter or keep traveling south if it gets colder. Starlings look different in the winter than they do in the summer. In the winter they have white speckles all over their bodies; in the summer the speckles are gone.

Grasshoppers can jump high and far. Their back legs are very strong. They jump away only if there's danger. Usually they stay put and trust in their camouflage. Grasshoppers can be as green as grass and as brown as a twig. You can hear grasshoppers when it's warm outside. They rub their long back legs against their wings, very fast. There are little bristles on their legs, and this makes a rasping sound. Many different kinds of grasshoppers can live in the garden.

The male **song thrush** looks just like the female. He searches for food in the grass and in the bushes. The song thrush loves to eat worms and slugs. He likes snails, too, but first he has to get past that shell. To do that he smashes the shell against a stone until it breaks. Now the song thrush can pull the snail out. Stones that are surrounded by lots of broken snail shells are called thrush's anvils.

The **water spider** lives under water. Sometimes you find them in garden ponds. A water spider can't breathe under water because it doesn't have gills, so it has to keep coming up for fresh air. When the spider goes under water it carries an air bubble between the hairs on the back of its body as a kind of air supply. If it spends more time under water it spins a web that it fills with air from the bottom. Then the spider sits inside and doesn't have to come out of the water for a while. From this spot it can hunt tadpoles and mosquito larvae.

Dragonflies are big insects that you see mostly in the summer. They have four big transparent wings and big eyes. Dragonflies lay their eggs in or near the water. They're hunters, and they catch their prey in the air. They fly much faster than you can bike, and they can even fly backwards. Dragonflies use a mask attached to their head to catch their prey. They unfold it and use it to bite the prey into pieces. Sometimes you see dragonflies that are stuck together. The one on top is the male, and the one on the bottom is the female. They're mating. Larvae crawl out of the eggs they lay. The larvae are raiders that search for food under water.

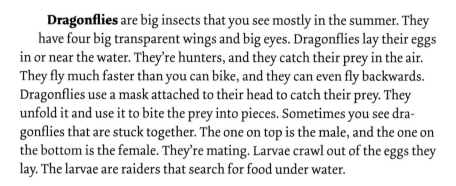

Lika falls right in, head over heels. When she comes back up she swims to the bank as fast as she can and shakes herself off.

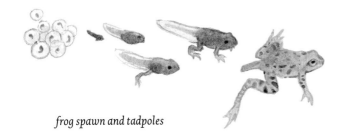

frog spawn and tadpoles

A **tadpole** has a tail and gills and swims in the water. Yet the tadpole isn't a real fish. It's the larva of a **frog**, and a frog is an amphibian. The mother frog lays her eggs in the water. This clump of eggs is called spawn. The tadpoles creep out of the eggs, and in a few weeks they develop back legs and then front legs. The tail gets smaller and smaller, and then the frog is complete. It's still much smaller than its parents.

You often see **gray herons** near canals and ponds. Herons like to eat the goldfish from garden ponds, too. A heron can empty a whole pond in one morning. Herons make their nests in trees. Early in the year they build a nest out of twigs. Gray herons brood in colonies, and you can smell them from far away. The bottom of the nest stinks from their excrement, which smells like fish. Sometimes you see a heron standing along the side of a canal with its wings hanging down. That doesn't mean it's sick; it's just sunbathing.

Goldfish are often kept in garden ponds. If the water is deep enough they can survive the winter. Goldfish come in many strange shapes, with big eyes and long fins. The unusual ones cost a lot of money. And if a gray heron happens to eat one... Goldfish originally come from China, Vietnam, and Japan. They were bred there a thousand years ago as ornamental fish. They're omnivores and can live to be fifteen years old.

Swallows arrive in the spring from the warm south and leave in the fall. Swallows build nests of mud and bits of plants, usually on a lath against the wall on the inside of a roof. They often brood in barns and stables, sometimes three times in a row. Swallows eat only insects, which they catch in mid-air while they're flying.

The **pipistrelle** is a small and common bat. You sometimes see them on summer evenings, flying in the glow of the streetlights in search of food. That's where the mosquitoes and moths can be found, which makes them easy prey for the pipistrelle. Some bats also come into people's houses, for instance the brown bat, the big-eared bat, and the pipistrelle.

The **wren** is one of the smallest birds. It can be heard everywhere, but it's not easy to spot. You can recognize a wren by its short tail, which stands almost straight up. This little bird makes a whole lot of noise. It can sing for a very long time, and very loudly.

Shrews look a little like mice, but they're not mice at all. Their teeth are completely different from those of the wood mouse or the house mouse. They're insect eaters. Real mice have teeth and molars for grinding up grain. Shrews have to eat all the time, day and night, or they won't get enough warmth. Shrews live in grass and leaves. Sometimes a shrew will wander into the house. Not many animals like to eat shrews. They have a disgusting smell and they taste nasty. Cats sometimes catch them, but they usually don't eat them.

The **woodworm** isn't really a worm. It's a beetle. It gets its name from the shape of its larvae, which look a little like worms. The beetles creep out of the wood in the summer. You can tell from the powder lying under the wood. In the wood there's a little round hole. The beetles can't live in houses with central heating because it isn't damp enough for them.

In the garden there's an old shed.
Lika curls up in the morning
sunshine so she can dry out and
rest from all her adventures.

Centipede means "a hundred legs," but the centipede doesn't have nearly that many. Its body is built up of rings. On each ring there are two legs, one on either side. The centipede is a carnivore. It likes to eat little insects that live in the house and garden. On its menu are wood lice, mites, and silverfish. Centipedes live in the ground, under stones and wood, and in piles of leaves. When a centipede crawls out of its egg it already has all its legs. The millipede doesn't. It gets another pair each time it sheds its skin, until it's full grown.

You'll find **brown rats** all over the world. The brown rat comes out only when it's dark. It crawls out of its hole and starts searching for food. It eats kitchen scraps: stale bread, vegetables, fruit, and bits of meat. A brown rat is very cautious. It won't run out into an open area but always makes its way around the edges. The brown rat is much larger than the house mouse. Its tail is as long as its body. It lives in dirty, damp places like sewers, so it can carry diseases to the human population.

Earwigs are very well known insects. They're brown creatures with big pincers on their rear end. They live in every garden and sometimes come in the house in the summer. Earwigs are nocturnal animals, and they eat everything. The female lays her eggs in a hole in the ground. When the eggs hatch, the mother cares for the young. The young quickly start searching for food on their own and wander farther and farther from the nest. Earwigs use their pincers to ward off danger. They like to crawl into dark holes, but they won't crawl into your ear – that's an old wives' tale.

The **slug** doesn't have a house for protection. So what does it do when an enemy comes around or the sun shines too brightly? It finds a good hiding place and comes out only when it's damp. When it rains you suddenly see the slimy trails left by slugs all over the place. When the rain stops they look for shelter again among the plants. A slug is both male and female at the same time. It doesn't mate with itself, though – only with other slugs. It takes two to three years before a slug grows into an adult, and it can live to be ten years old.

The male **blackbird** is black and has an orange beak. The female is brown and has a dark beak. Male blackbirds start quarreling early in the spring. They all want their own place and their own female. They start singing as soon as the sun comes up and can keep singing for up to an hour. In the evening they start singing again, just before it's dark. They do this to let the other blackbirds know who's boss in the garden. Once the blackbirds know whose garden is whose, they stop quarreling. They mate with a female instead and build a nest. When the eggs hatch, both parents care for the young, who get mostly worms to eat.

female blackbird

Lika walks past the compost heap.
She sniffs a bit and looks for any
tasty tidbits.

What's that rustling?
There under the bushes –
something's moving! Step by step,
Lika gets closer and closer.

Plant lice are never alone. They live on plants in big colonies. Plant lice drink plant sap to stay alive. Whatever they can't use, they expel as poop. The poop is sticky because there's a lot of sugar in it. Ants love plant lice. The ant strokes the rear of the plant louse with its antennae. This makes the plant louse poop, which is just what the ant wants: a nice sweet meal.

Actually the **robin redbreast** has the wrong name. If you look carefully you'll see that the bird's color is quite different . The males and females are identical. They may look friendly, but they're not. They can be pretty quarrelsome and sometimes they even fight. Robins live most of the year alone, but during the breeding season they live in pairs. Sometimes robins tap against the window, mistaking their reflection for an intruder. They tap with their beak to chase the intruder away. Tap tap tap, tap against the window...

The **garden spider** is the most common of all the spiders. In the spring you see them in every garden. A garden spider always hangs upside down. The big garden spiders are the females. The males are quite a bit smaller. The male has to be very careful if he wants to mate. Far too often the female will mistake the male for prey. The male often brings a tasty tidbit for the female as a distraction. If the female is willing, the two spiders mate. Then the male has to make a quick getaway if he doesn't want to be eaten.

Is there anyone who's never seen the little beetle with the red-orange wing-case and black dots?

ladybugs and a larva; these beetles come in many varieties and different colors

There are 5000 varieties of **ladybugs** worldwide. The most familiar are those with two dots and those with seven dots. The red color sends a warning to predators, such as birds: watch out, I'm poisonous. If the ladybird is attacked it produces a yellow, nasty-smelling liquid. Most birds will then leave the ladybug alone. If the bird keeps on attacking, the ladybug can do one more thing: play dead and hope that the bird flies away.

You're not likely to run into a **hedgehog** in the daytime. When evening arrives, the hedgehog comes out of hiding and starts looking for food. Hedgehogs eat worms, snails, and all kinds of insects. With their sharp teeth they can bite through the hard wing-cases of beetles and bugs. When a hedgehog is threatened, it rolls up in a ball. That way it protects its soft belly and its head. Its quills keep attackers at bay. The hedgehog hibernates and doesn't eat anything all winter long. It doesn't wake up until the weather starts getting warmer. Then it quickly eats as much as it can, to put back all the weight it lost during the winter.

Lika feels like climbing a tree.
She stretches out her body and
sets her claws firmly in the bark.
Three seconds later she's on top
of the birdhouse. Up fly the birds,
chirping loudly. Danger!

male house sparrow

great titmouse
and bluetit

Great titmice and **bluetits** like to nest in birdhouses. Great titmice are stronger than bluetits, and they chase the bluetits away. But if you want bluetits to brood in your birdhouse, you have to make the opening small enough so that only a bluetit can fit in. It takes a week or two before the tit eggs hatch. Then the tit parents have lots of work to do. They fly back and forth with food. Sometimes it's a caterpillar and sometimes a butterfly. Once the parents have fed their young they carry out the youngsters' poop in their beaks. The poop is neatly packaged in a thin membrane so it all stays together.

black crow

jackdaw

rook

House sparrows live wherever people are living. The males and females look quite different. House sparrows usually brood under roofing tiles. They feed their young in the summer with insects. For the rest of the year they're omnivores. In recent years there have been fewer house sparrows than there used to be. No one knows why.

female house sparrow

A **black crow** is just as big as a **rook**. Both of them are completely black, and both have strong beaks. The rook's head is bald at the front; the crow's is covered with black feathers. You usually see black crows in pairs or with their young. You can spot them in gardens and in every city park. Rooks always travel in groups. They live in colonies, and you can hear them from far away. **Jackdaws** are smaller than black crows and are not completely black. They have a gray nape and light-colored eyes. Jackdaws are also sometimes called grackles.

The **Eurasian jay** stocks up food in the fall. The acorns that fall from the trees are more than it can handle. The jay hides dozens of them in the ground in case it gets hungry in the winter. Usually it remembers where it has hidden them, but sometimes it forgets. That's good, too, because the forgotten acorns grown into new trees in the spring. In the middle of the winter you occasionally see the Eurasian jay eating from city bird feeders. That means it's really hungry, because normally these birds don't like to get too close to people.

Magpies start working on their nests at the end of the winter. That's when they look their best, all dressed up in gleaming robes of feathers. Their long tail sometimes appears green and sometimes black, depending on how the sun strikes it. Later in the year you see magpies in groups: parents with their fledgling young. Magpies like to eat dead animals, worms, snails, and caterpillars. But they also like to eat the eggs and young of other birds. They know where the blackbirds and song thrushes have built their nests. If those birds aren't careful, the magpies will grab their young as quick as lightning.

Earthworms live most of their lives underground. They eat a path through the soil. With their intestines they remove whatever they can use, and they poop the rest out. You've probably seen the gray piles of poop lying between the blades of grass. Worms look smooth, but they're not. Their bodies are covered with tiny, stiff hairs. They use them when they dig to push themselves through their tunnels. Most worms have a thick segment on their bodies called a saddle. It's not a wound. Inside that thick, light pink segment are the worm's eggs. A worm is both male and female, and it can make both eggs and sperm. It doesn't fertilize itself, though. Another worm has to do that. If part of a worm breaks off, it just grows back.

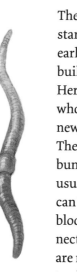

The **bumblebee** queen starts making her nest early in the spring. She builds it from bits of plants. Her first eggs produce workers, who help the queen. Later in the year new queens and males are born. There are far fewer animals in a bumblebee colony than in a beehive – usually about a hundred. Bumblebees can be found wherever flowers are blooming. They collect pollen and nectar for their colony. Bumblebees are not quick to sting. They're much too busy looking for food.

The **snail** carries its shell on its back. Its house is attached to its body, and the snail can crawl right into it. Snails do that in the summer when it's very warm. Once they're inside, they shut the opening of the shell with a layer of slime, which keeps them from drying out. They can live for weeks that way without having to eat or drink. Most species have beautifully colored shells. They're yellow, brown, or pink, often with dark stripes, thick or thin. The snails themselves are pretty dull: plain old gray.

Toads sleep all winter long. They come out in the spring when it gets warmer. Then they leave their winter habitat and go to the place where they lay their eggs. The toad has glands that produce bad-smelling liquid when danger threatens. A predator would think twice before eating a toad. Not only does a toad stink, but it tastes nasty, too. If a toad feels threatened, sometimes it stands way up on its legs. If all else fails, the toad makes a run for it.

The **mole** has a body that's perfect for living underground. It never comes out. It uses its long claws to dig tunnels, its whiskers to find earthworms. It can see hardly anything with its weak eyes, but the mole ends up just where it wants to be by feeling its way. A molehill is the earth that's left after the mole has finished its excavation work. Whatever it wants to get rid of, it just pushes out.

Lika walks into the vegetable garden.
Suddenly the earth under her feet starts
rising. Lika steps aside and looks at the dark
mound with surprise. She scratches away
a bit of earth, but the mole has already
disappeared.

Lika is back in the house. Tired from all her adventures, she lies down on the chair. She stretches herself and yawns. "Just look at that lazy cat," says Father when he comes downstairs a little while later. "How nice it must be to sleep all day long." Lika opens her right eye and quickly shuts it again. It's just as if she were winking…